World of R

A 3-in-1 Listen-Along Rea

Disney Junior

Best Day Ever!

Three Fun Tales

DISNEY PRESS
Los Angeles • New York

Pups on a Mission, First Paperback Edition, September 2018.
Mickey's Perfecto Day, First Paperback Edition, October 2017.
Vampirina in the Fall, First Paperback Edition, June 2018.

First Paperback Edition, March 2020
1 3 5 7 9 10 8 6 4 2

ISBN 978-1-368-04497-4
FAC-029261-20045
Library of Congress Control Number: 2019946379

Printed in the United States of America

For more Disney Press fun, visit www.disneybooks.com

SUSTAINABLE
FORESTRY
INITIATIVE
Certified Sourcing
www.sfiprogram.org
SFI-01415

Pups on a
MISSION

Adapted by Lori Froeb

Based on the series created by Harland Williams

Illustrated by the Disney Storybook Art Team

Bob is home!
Bingo and Rolly are happy to see him.
They bark. They wag their tails.
Bob says, "Let's play ball."

The puppies do not
know where their ball is.

Bob does not know where their ball is, either.

Hissy thinks she saw the ball in the kitchen.
The pups run to the kitchen.

The ball is not by the toaster.

The ball is not in the fridge.

The pups run to the living room.
The ball is not under the pillows.
The ball is not on the bookshelf.

The pups make a mess.
A.R.F. cleans up the mess.
The pups still cannot find the ball.

The pups have a mission:
FIND THEIR BALL!
Bingo and Rolly collar up.

They run to the backyard.
They look in the sandbox.
The ball is not in the sandbox.

The gopher thinks he saw the ball at the dog park.

Bingo and Rolly run to the dog park.

The pups look inside the tube slide.
They do not find the ball.
They find Cupcake.

Cupcake thinks she saw a
big dog with their ball.

Bingo and Rolly find the big dog.
She does not have their ball.

The big dog thinks the squirrel has their ball.

The pups find the squirrel.
He does not have their ball.

The squirrel thinks he saw
their ball at the farm.

Rolly and Bingo run to the farm.
The ball is not in the pigpen.

The ball is not in the henhouse.

The puppies are sad.
Where can their ball be?

The pups see a bird.
The bird thinks he saw the ball
at the beach.

The pups run to the beach.
Bingo looks for the ball.
Rolly looks at a crab.

Rolly digs and digs.

Rolly digs some more.
Bingo spots a boat.

"That boat looks like our bath toy," says Bingo.

"We play with bath toys in the bathtub," says Rolly.

"We play with our ball in the bathtub, too," Bingo says.

The pups run home.
They know just where to look.

Their ball is right where they left it.
It is in the tub!

Mission accomplished! Time to play ball.

MICKEY'S PERFECTO DAY!

Adapted by **SHERRI STONER**

Based on the episode written by **ASHLEY MENDOZA**

Illustrated by **LOTER, INC.**

Mickey and his pals pack for a trip.
They are going to Madrid, Spain.
They will see the sights.
Donald will sing with his friends.
It will be a *perfecto* day!

The gang drives their Daily Drivers to Madrid.

They pass a baby bull sniffing a rose.
The rose falls off the bush.
It lands in Minnie's car!

Minnie puts the rose behind her ear.
The baby bull runs after his rose.
Minnie does not notice.

The gang gets to Spain.
Mickey and Minnie go to the market.
It is a *perfecto* day!
The baby bull follows his nose
to the rose.

Minnie shops.

Minnie tries on dresses.

The baby bull sniffs the rose.

Minnie does not notice.

But Mickey notices!
"B-b-b-bull!" Mickey shouts.

Mickey and Minnie jump into a cart.
It rolls away from the bull.
It rolls into . . .

. . . a churro cart!

"We'll take two," says Mickey.

Donald finds his friends.
They invite Daisy and Donald
to lunch.
It is a *perfecto* day!

Donald tries the potatoes.
"AAAACK!" he shouts.
They are very spicy.

Daisy tries to help.
She gives him water to drink.

It's almost time to sing.
The group warms up.
Donald opens his mouth.
No sound comes out.

Who will sing at the show?
Donald's friends ask Daisy to sing!

Donald is sad he can't sing with
his friends.
He gives Daisy his hat.

Poor Donald.
His friend brings him dessert.
He will watch the show from
his table.

Mickey and Minnie visit the plaza.
The bull visits the plaza, too.

He follows his nose to the rose.
Mickey and Minnie run!

The friends find a spot
to hide in.
The baby bull runs right
by them.

Mickey and Minnie run to the show.
Daisy is singing with the band.

Donald finishes dessert.
He gets the bill.
"WHAT?" he shouts.
His voice is back!

Donald joins the band.

They sing together.

The crowd loves the show!

The baby bull comes to the show, too.
He sits next to Minnie.
He sniffs her rose.

"He just likes my flower!" Minnie says.
She gives the bull her rose.
The bull gives Mickey a kiss!

Minnie giggles.
What a *perfecto* day!

Disney Junior

Vampirina

VAMPIRINA
in the
FALL

Written by SARA MILLER

Illustrated by IMAGINISM STUDIO

and the DISNEY STORYBOOK ART TEAM

Vampirina loves all the seasons.

She loves winter.

She loves spring.

She loves summer.

But of them all, Vee's favorite
season is . . . fall!

In the fall, Vee goes back to school!

Vee's batpack holds her
school supplies.

In the fall, the Woodchuck
Woodsies go leaf-peeping.

The Woodsies have bake sales, too.
Vee sells her mummy-bear cookies
and flying batcakes.

Vee goes apple picking
in the fall.

She makes creepy candy apples, spooky spiced cider, and wormy apple pie!

The weather starts getting
colder in the fall.

It reminds Vee of eerie nights in Transylvania.

And in the fall, Nanpire knits cozy sweaters for everyone.

Fall is for jumping in piles of crunchy leaves!

Fall is for camping.
And fall is for telling spooky
stories around the campfire.

Fall is for Halloween!
Vee's family hangs lots of cobwebs.

They put spooky cauldrons in every corner.

And they make
sure the treat
bowls are
always full.

Vee's friends dress up in
Halloween costumes!
But Vampirina does not need one.
She gets to be herself!

Fall is also for Fangsgiving!
Chef Remy Bones cooks
for days and days.

Vee loves the cobweb stuffing and the monster mashed potatoes.

Her favorite is the pumpkin pie
with ghoul whip on top!

But guess what Vee likes most of all.
Being with her family in the fall!